turned   f the
vn

SHARK
IN THE DARK

About the author and illustrator:

Peter Bently has written many picture books, and won
awards for them too! He enjoys visiting schools and libraries where
he shares his stories with children – but not before he's tried them out
on his family. Peter is very fond of fish (especially with chips).

Ben Cort is the bestselling, award-winning illustrator of over eighty
books for children – and he's written one too. Ben has swum the
Great Barrier Reef in Australia and although he didn't see
a shark there, he did spot a sea slug!

First published 2008 by Macmillan Children's Books
This edition published 2014 by Macmillan Children's Books
a division of Macmillan Publishers Limited
20 New Wharf Road, London N1 9RR
Basingstoke and Oxford
Associated companies throughout the world
www.panmacmillan.com

ISBN: 978-1-4472-3696-2

Text copyright © Peter Bently 2008
Illustrations copyright © Ben Cort 2008
Moral rights asserted

2 4 6 8 9 7 5 3 1

A CIP catalogue record for this book is available from the British Library.

Printed in China

THE SHARK IN THE DARK

Peter Bently

Illustrated by Ben Cort

MACMILLAN CHILDREN'S BOOKS

Down at the bottom of the deep, dark sea,
Something is stirring and it wants its tea.
His teeth are like knives and his eyes small and beady,
He's big and he's mean and he's terribly greedy.

Watch out, little fishes, watch out for the Shark!
Watch out for the great hungry

Shark in the Dark!

The flounders were floundering.
"Here comes the Shark!"

The turtles were terrified.
"Here comes the Shark!"

"Oh help!" moaned the mackerel.
"The Shark's on his way!
We don't want to be in his belly today!"

And all of the fishes were flustered and bumbling —
"Here comes the Shark and his tummy is rumbling!"

"Now fish," smiled the Shark,
    "it's been ages since lunch,
I just want a wee fishy something to munch.

Just the tiniest, tastiest, fishiest snack,
So please," grinned the Shark in the Dark . . .

" . . . Hey, come back!"

"No way!" cried the crabs.
    "We don't mean to sound selfish,
But inside a shark is no place for a shellfish."
"That's right," cried the cod. "We don't want to be tea.
Please go back, Mister Shark, to the dark of the sea!"

"Oh I will," sneered the Shark,
"when I've had a few shoals
For my tea. Or fresh lobsters perhaps?
Or some soles?"

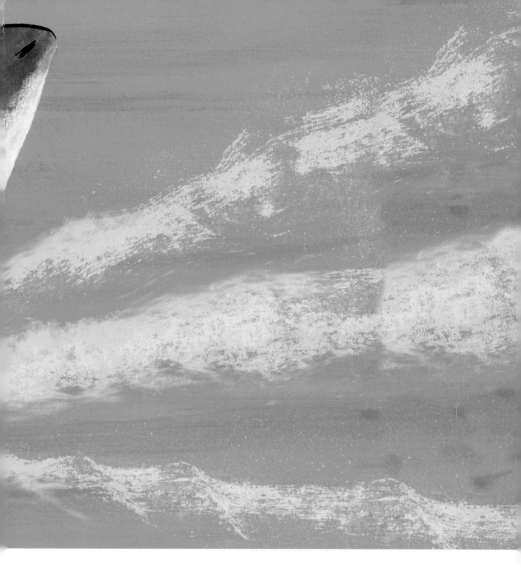

And he opened his jaws and his laughter was manic,
And put all the fish in a terrible panic.

Away swam the fish, all desperate to hide
Far from the Shark with his jaws open wide.
"Hello!" said a squid. "What's going on here?
What's all this fussing, what is there to fear?"

"HELP!" flapped the fish. "We're afraid of the Shark,
The big greedy Shark who lives in the dark.
He's coming to eat us, he's coming right now!
How can we keep him away, tell us, how?"

"I see," frowned the Squid.
　　"So the Shark thinks it's clever
To push you around cos he's bigger than you.

Well, I've got a plan which will make sure he never
Swims this way again. Now, here's what we'll do . . ."

So, along swam the Shark and he peered all around
With his mean, beady eyes —
    but no fish could be found.

"That's funny," he grumbled.
    "Where have they all gone?"
They can't all have vanished, like that, every one?"

And then, in the distance, he saw a dim shape.
"Aha!" thought the Shark.
"THIS small fish won't escape!"

But the closer that fish got, the bigger it grew.
And it grew . . . and it grew . . .
into something he knew.

The shadowy head and the shadowy tail,
And the gigantic wide-open jaws of a . . .

. . . WHALE!

"Hey Shark!" boomed the Whale.
    "Come right here, little fish!
I'm peckish — you're small but you'll do for a dish.

I've come a long way, I need food in my tummy,
A dinner of shark sounds delicious and scrummy!"

With a shiver and shudder
  the Shark wailed, "Oh heck!
There's no way that I'm going to
  swim down your neck!"

And then with a flick and a flash of his fin,
The Shark shouted "Bye!" with a half-hearted grin.

And back to the dark fled the Shark in a fright,
As the Whale swam slowly out into the light . . .

"You see," laughed the Squid, "when we all got together,

We taught him a thing he'll remember forever!"

THE SHARK IN THE DARK

FASCINATING SHARK FACTS

The Shark in the Dark is a Great White Shark, one of the fiercest sharks of all.

Great Whites have three rows of very sharp teeth which fall out and grow back all the time. Some sharks go through 30,000 teeth in a lifetime!

As well as ferocious hunters, the shark family includes gentle giants like Basking Sharks and the weird-looking Hammerhead Shark.

From **little** . . . some sharks are small enough to hold in your hands, like the Spined Pygmy Shark, which can be as tiny as 15cm, and the Dwarf Dogfish, which is about 16cm long.

. . . to **large.** The Whale Shark is the biggest fish in the world. It can grow up to 15 metres long and has a mouth so wide you could drive a car into it!

Endangered!
More than 100 species of shark are in danger of extinction. This is because humans hunt sharks for food, accidentally trap them in nets, and destroy places where they live.